"NAME THE GREATEST OF ALL INVENTORS: ACCIDENT."

Mark Twain

34 4124 0011 3007

TO JON,
WITH LOVE.

First published 2017 by Nosy Crow Ltd
The Crow's Nest, 10a Lant Street
London SE1 1QR
www.nosycrow.com

ISBN 978 0 85763 820 5 (HB)
ISBN 978 0 85763 824 3 (PB)

Nosy Crow and associated logos are trademarks
and/or registered trademarks of Nosy Crow Ltd.

Text and illustration © Frann Preston-Gannon 2017

The right of Frann Preston-Gannon to be identified as the author
and illustrator of this work has been asserted.

Printed in China by Imago
Papers used by Nosy Crow are made from wood grown in sustainable forests.

1 3 5 7 9 8 6 4 2 (HB)
1 3 5 7 9 8 6 4 2 (PB)

DAVE'S ROCK

FRANN PRESTON-GANNON

nosy crow

This Dave.

Dave **love** rock.

Jon **love** rock, too.

Dave's rock **bigger**.

Jon's rock **faster.**

Dave find
new rock.

New rock
prettier.

Dave's rock
not rock.

Jon's rock **taller.**

Dave **not** happy . . .

. . . but Jon have **idea!**

Jon make rock
better.

Dave make rock
better, too.

Look! Rocks same. Nice and round.
Matching rocks give Dave idea!

Dave find stick.
Rock make fun game!

Jon and Dave **happy** . . .

. . . friends happy, too.